For our Paul

First published in the United Kingdom in 2005

This paperback edition first published in the United Kingdom in 2017 by
Pavilion Children's Books
43 Great Ormond Street, London, WC1N 3HZ

An imprint of Pavilion Books Group Limited

Produced by Breslich & Foss Ltd

A CIP catalogue record for this book is available from the British Library.

ISBN 9781843653288

Reproduction by Mission Productions, Hong Kong
Printed by Toppan Leefung Printing Ltd, China

10 9 8 7 6 5 4 3 2 1

This book can be ordered online direct from the publisher at:
www.pavilionbooks.com, or try your local bookshop.

Little Red

A howlingly good fairy tale with a twist

RETOLD BY LYNN ROBERTS-MALONEY

ILLUSTRATED BY DAVID ROBERTS

PAVILION

In a time not too long ago and in a land much like our own, there lived a young boy. His name was Thomas, but – for some reason – everyone called him Little Red.

Little Red's parents owned a cosy inn, and people came from far and wide for a glass of their famous sweet ginger beer. Little Red loved to meet the travellers and hear their tales of dangerous encounters with dashing highwaymen and fearsome wolves.

One day Little Red was getting ready to visit his grandma, as he did every week, with a basketful of delicious treats and a week's supply of ginger beer.

"Grandma's favourite," declared Little Red, as he put the keg of ginger beer in his basket.

Little Red put on his much-loved red coat, picked up his basket, and set off for Grandma's.

As always, his mother warned him, "Don't you wander off the path, not for *any* reason." For everyone knew that a ferocious and hungry wolf prowled within the forest and straying from the path would almost certainly mean being eaten!

Little Red skipped along the path unaware the wolf was secretly watching him. "He would make a tasty snack," the wolf said to himself, drooling at the thought.

Suddenly Little Red stopped and called out excitedly, "Red apples!
I'll have to take some for Grandma."

Overhearing this, the wolf thought, "So Grandma is waiting for him,
is she? Perhaps I can have myself two tasty snacks, instead of just one."

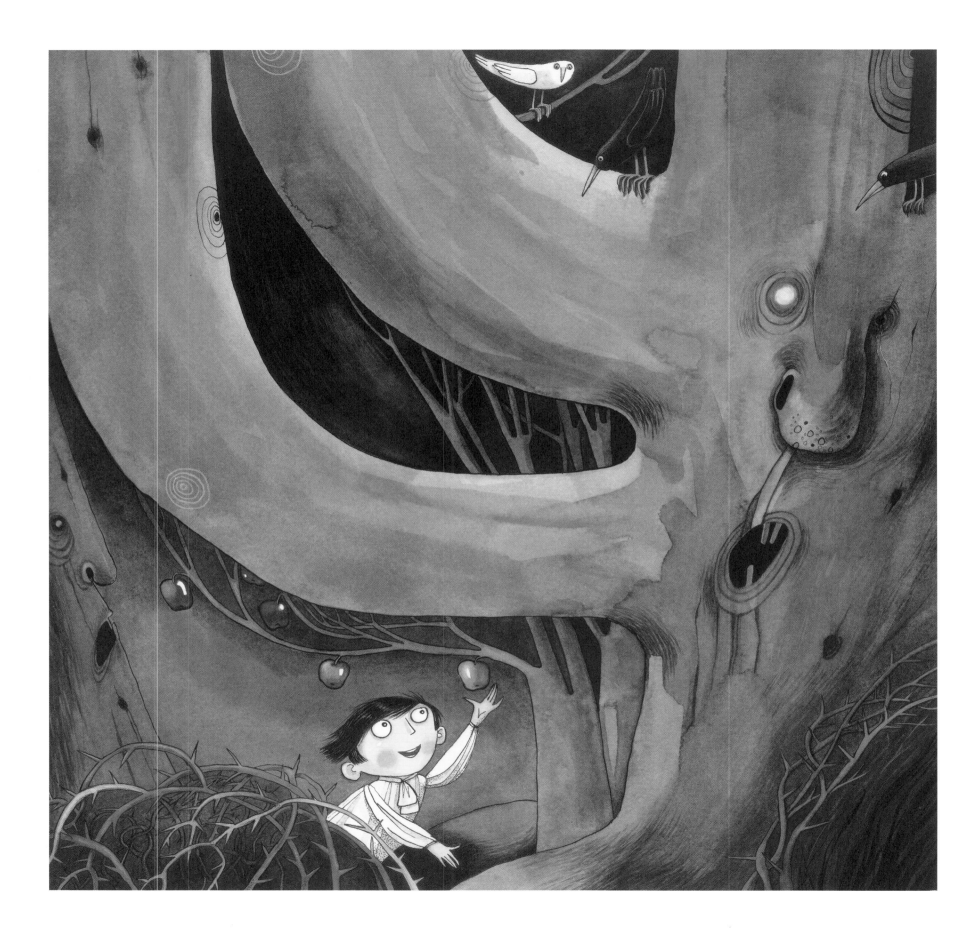

Meanwhile, Little Red was trying to reach the apples. There was a large prickly bush in his way, so to keep his coat from being torn, he took it off and placed it on a nearby rock.

This gave the wolf an idea. Grabbing the coat, he charged off at a terrific pace to Grandma's house.

Reaching Grandma's front door, the wolf stopped to squeeze himself into Little Red's coat. Then he knocked on the door.

Grandma, who was very, *very* shortsighted, opened the door, saw the red jacket, and said, "Come right in, Little Red. Why don't we have some ginger beer and a big slice of cake?"

But as soon as her back was turned, the wolf pounced on her, and in one second flat, he had swallowed her whole!

"Now I'll disguise myself as Grandma and eat the boy for dessert," the wolf howled, marvelling at his brilliant plan. He stepped into one of Grandma's dresses and fixed one of her wigs behind his long furry ears. He closed the drapes tight, sat at Grandma's table and waited eagerly for Little Red.

Little Red arrived at Grandma's house out of breath from running.

"Grandma," he cried, "my coat has been stolen! I only left the path for a second, and it disappeared."

When Grandma didn't rush out to greet him, Little Red began to worry. "Are you in there?" he asked, stepping into the darkened room.

"Grandma," he said, "you look different. Are you feeling unwell?"

"I'm fine, dear," said the wolf sweetly. "Come closer."

"Grandma, what big eyes you've got today," said Little Red, sitting down at the table.

"All the better to see you with, my dear," crooned the wolf.

"But what big ears you have, Grandma," Little Red said.

"All the better to hear you with, my sweet," replied the wolf with a big toothy grin.

"And, Grandma, what enormous teeth you have!" Little Red exclaimed.

"All the better to eat you with!" roared the wolf.

"What?" cried Little Red. "Don't eat *me*!"

"You're my dessert," growled the wolf. "Grandma was really delicious but not quite enough to fill me up. You'll finish the meal off nicely."

Terrified, Little Red looked around frantically for a way out. Then he remembered his basket and had a brilliant idea.

"Wait! I have something much, much tastier than me," shouted Little Red and he grabbed the keg of ginger beer from his basket.

"Tastier than you?" thundered the wolf.

Snatching the bottle from Little Red's hand, the wolf guzzled down the whole lot – enough for an entire week! – in one greedy gulp.

Almost immediately, the wolf's belly began to rumble and grumble loudly.

"Oh dear, oh dear, oh dear!" the wolf
howled. Then suddenly, he let
out an enormous burp and
out flew Grandma
from his mouth!

belch!

As the wolf tottered backwards, groaning, Little Red grabbed the empty keg of ginger beer and threw it at the wolf's head, knocking him out cold. Then he quickly tied a pair of Grandma's thick woolly stockings tightly around the wolf's paws.

The wolf awoke with a nasty bump on his head. "My poor, poor head," he moaned. "Eating grandmas is becoming much too dangerous! And that ginger beer was far tastier than Grandma anyway."

That gave Little Red an idea. "If you promise never to eat anyone ever again," he said, "I'll let you go and make sure you have all the ginger beer you could ever want."

The wolf readily agreed. So from then on, each week on his way to Grandma's, Little Red left a keg of ginger beer in the forest for the wolf, who drank it down eagerly, in spite of its embarrassing aftereffects!

The End

Illustrator's Note

After exploring the 1930s for our first fairy tale, *Cinderella*, and reminiscing over the 1970s in our second, *Rapunzel*, Lynn and I decided to travel back to the late eighteenth century for *Little Red*, as we wanted this retelling to have a feeling of danger, drama, and suspense. The dark and menacing forest with strange faces in the trees seemed a perfect setting for our sly, scheming wolf to prowl. And the eighteenth-century style of big wigs, satin gowns, beauty spots, powdered faces, and highwaymen fits well alongside it. I researched both European and early American furniture and clothing for this tale, as I envisaged Little Red's family to be English pioneers to the new century. Grandma is rather stylish and well-to-do and you may recognize a famous painting or two in her house, along with her imported Delft earthernware. Also, if you look very closely, you will find a couple of references to *Cinderella*!

The illustrations were done in pen and ink with watercolour on hot-pressed, heavyweight paper.